THE CURSE OF THE CATASTROPHIC CUPCAKES

Peter Millett was born in New Zealand. He was first published aged nine when one of his humorous poems appeared in the national press. He has since gone on to publish a great many children's books in New Zealand, including picture books and educational books. He has a passion for zany English humour and Spike Milligan is one of his all-time heroes. He lives with his family in Auckland.

Also available

THE PETRIFYING PLOT OF
THE PLUMMETING PANTS

THE ATTACK OF THE BRAIN-DEAD
BREAKDANCING ZOMBIES

BOY ZERO
WANNABE HERO

THE CURSE OF THE CATASTROPHIC CUPCAKES

Peter Millett

Illustrations by Steve May

ff

faber and faber

FOR ROOM 16

First published in 2011 by
Faber and Faber Limited
Bloomsbury House, 74–77 Great Russell Street,
London, WC1B 3DA

Typeset by Faber and Faber
Printed in England by CPI BookMarque, Croydon

A CIP record for this book
is available from the British Library

ISBN 978–0–571–25326–5

2 4 6 8 10 9 7 5 3 1

CONTENTS

AUTHOR NOTE

This book was written for lovers of baked beans and poetry.

THE CURSE OF THE CRUMPLED COSTUME

Charlie Applejack, the world's newest and most unusual superhero, paced about nervously in his bedroom. He felt his pulse race and his knuckles begin to whiten. He was about to face his most terrifying challenge yet – public speaking!

Josh, his best friend, looked up over his PSP. 'So, Charlie, have you finished writing your acceptance speech for the award ceremony yet? You've been at it for ever – you're going to burn a hole in the carpet if you keep circling like that.'

Charlie frowned. 'Honestly, Josh, I can't think of anything to say.'

Josh sat up. 'Well, what have you written so far?'

Charlie cleared his throat. 'Um . . . Hi, I'm Hero

Boy. Thanks for coming. I hope your seats are comfortable . . .'

Josh dropped his PSP on the bed. 'Is that it? That's rubbish,' he groaned. 'Listen, you're about to be awarded the Junior Superhero of the Year trophy. You can't open your speech with *are your seats comfortable!'*

Charlie scratched his nose. 'Um, how about I begin with a "knock-knock" joke instead?'

'Urgh!' Josh buried his face in a pillow. 'C'mon . . . just tell them all the secrets of how to be a superhero.'

'But Josh, I don't know any secrets about being a superhero. I've never had any training, I've never been to Super School – and I'm still hopeless at flying! Look, I might have saved the world from General Pandemonium two times already, but I don't really have a clue how I did it!'

'Urgh,' Josh groaned again.

Suddenly – **WRRONGGG** – a dark shadow passed by Charlie's window.

'Huh?' Charlie gasped.

Josh rushed over to the window. 'Hey, Charlie – look, your super shuttle's arrived!'

Charlie glanced at his watch. 'What? Already? They're way earlier than I thought they would be. I haven't even got my costume ready yet.'

'Well get it on quick, then,' Josh urged. 'We've gotta go.'

Charlie furiously rifled through his bedroom cupboard. 'Where is it? Where is it?' he bleated, throwing his clothes across the floor. He leaned out into the hallway. 'Mum, help! I can't find my costume anywhere – and the super shuttle's come to pick me up!'

Mum rushed in. 'All right, let's think. Where did you last put it?'

'In a box in the bottom of this cupboard.'

Mum arched her eyebrows. 'Oh, is that where you store your costume? I thought that tatty old box was full of rubbish, so I threw it out when I was tidying up this morning. I asked you to do it yesterday but—'

'No – this isn't happening!' Charlie raced down the stairs and out into the backyard. He lifted the

lid off the rubbish bin and saw his costume lying under a pile of rotting banana skins, vegetable peelings and sticky chewing-gum wrappers.

'Urgh . . .' he groaned as he pulled out his costume – which consisted of a shower curtain, cleaning gloves, goggles and swimming cap – and gingerly slipped them on.

He then sprinted back into the hallway and shouted up the staircase. 'C'mon, everybody – we've gotta leave right now.'

Josh skipped down the stairs with Dad following quickly behind him.

A few moments later Mum appeared, with Charlie's sister Trixie trudging slowly behind her.

'Do I really have to go to this stupid thing?' Trixie grumbled.

Dad smiled. 'Sweetie, take a leaf out of my number-one bestselling book *Never Ever Say Never Never – Ever Again* and try to enjoy a new experience. I'm sure it will be more fun than you imagine. Hey, you might even get to meet Turbo Troy there if you're lucky.'

Trixie sneered. 'Duh – he's a dork.'

Mum patted Trixie's head. 'But honey, won't it be a thrill to see your big brother up there on the stage receiving his award?'

Trixie sneered again. 'He's an even bigger dork.'

Charlie was hopping impatiently from one foot to the other. 'Can we *please* just go!' he said, and sprinted outside towards the waiting shuttle.

THE SERIOUSLY SCARY SUPER SPEECH

Fifteen minutes later the super shuttle touched down at the Hoogenheimer Centre where the award ceremony was being held. Charlie and Josh were the first out and they were quickly led away to a small room backstage, while Mum, Dad and Trixie were shown to their seats in the auditorium.

Charlie paced about anxiously in the small room while he waited to go on stage.

Josh looked at his watch. 'Okay, so have you worked out what you're going to say?'

Charlie shook his head. 'Nup. Not a word.'

Just then, Dad poked his head into the room. 'Hey, Son, I thought I'd just pop by and wish you all the best – I can't wait to hear your big speech.'

Charlie frowned. 'B–but, Dad, I don't know what I'm going to say. I'm t–too nervous to speak in front of all those real superheroes.'

Dad grinned. 'Don't worry, my boy; let me give you some super advice from my award-winning book *How to Fight Fear By Not Fighting Fair*. If you're feeling nervous today, just imagine that your audience is sitting in their underwear – I guarantee you'll relax in a flash,' he said, clicking his fingers.

Charlie furrowed his brow. 'But Dad – I'm going to be speaking in front of a bunch of people wearing superhero costumes; they *will* be sitting there in their underwear!'

Dad paused for a moment. 'Ahh . . .'

A man dressed in a silver suit entered the room.
'Okay, Zero Boy, it's time to receive your award,'
he said, signalling to Charlie.

Charlie groaned. 'Er, my name is actually Hero
Boy . . .'

Dad gave Charlie the thumbs up. 'Knock 'em
dead, Son,' he chirped as he scooted back off
towards the auditorium.

Charlie followed the silver-suited man through
a parting in an enormous pair of curtains.

Hooray!

A noisy cheer went up as Charlie walked
onto the stage. He looked to his left and saw
Commander Ron, the world's greatest superhero,
standing with a huge shiny trophy tucked under
his muscular arm.

The burly superhero saluted Charlie. 'Hero Boy,
it is my honour and privilege to present you with
the Junior Superhero of the Year award!'

Hooray!

Another roar went up as the crowd rose to their

feet and cheered wildly.

Commander Ron handed Charlie the trophy.
'Son . . . well done on winning this prestigious
award!' He shook Charlie's hand firmly. 'Tell us,'
he boomed, 'what's the secret of your success?
What makes you such an incredible young
superhero?'

He stepped back, leaving Charlie alone in the
centre of the stage. Charlie turned to the audience
and gulped loudly. 'Ummm . . .'

But suddenly – **WROOP WROOP WROOP
WROOP WROOP WROOP WROOP WROOP
WROOP** – a deafening alarm started ringing out.

A thundering voice echoed over the sound system.

'Superheroes of the world – alert stations – General Pandemonium has escaped from jail! I repeat, superheroes of the world – alert stations – General Pandemonium has escaped from jail!'

Commander Ron's jaw dropped.

WOOSH! ZOOM! SPONGG! The auditorium quickly began to empty as the superheroes rocketed out through the emergency doors.

Charlie looked blankly at the trophy in his hands.

Commander Ron clenched his fists. 'I can't believe it. How did this happen?'

He bent down and stared Charlie in the eye. 'Son, this is an absolute tragedy – your moment of glory has been ruined by that scumbag. I'm so sorry, but you won't be able to deliver your speech.' He gripped Charlie's shoulder. 'I bet that makes your blood boil, doesn't it.? You probably spent hours putting it together, and now no one's going to hear it. Oh, it must be heartbreaking.'

Charlie shrugged his shoulders and smiled politely. 'Don't worry, Commander Ron. I'll get over it.'

THE RISE OF THE SINISTER SNOWFLAKE

One week later . . .

On the top of a mist-covered mountain in the middle of a remote jungle, a frail old man with a long gingery beard sat quietly humming to himself.

'*A-um – a-um – a-um,*' he mumbled under his

breath. Suddenly his ears pricked up. He turned to his left and noticed a huge beak-like nose piercing through the early morning cloud below him.

The massive honker belonged to the recently escaped villain, General Pandemonium.

'Master Sushi – at last, I have found you . . .' the general puffed.

The wise old master stared at the general and instantly a look of pain spread across his face.

'Master Sushi, what's wrong?' the general cried. 'What causes you such discomfort?'

The frail old man weakly stood up, wobbling unsteadily. 'Master Sushi sit here for three days now and both feet fall fast asleep.' He shook out his right leg. 'Very hard to wake up. Now each toe feel like cushion that someone stick a thousand pins and needles in.' He glared at the general. 'Anyway, who are you and why you come here?'

'Master Sushi – I am General Pandemonium, the galaxy's most sensational supervillain. I come here urgently seeking your legendary evil wisdom.'

Master Sushi nodded. 'Ah, yes, General Mandy Pony Ian, I have heard of you – Master Sudoku speaks of you often.'

The general frowned. 'No – I said my name is Pan-de-mo-ni-um!'

Master Sushi smiled blankly. 'Whatever . . .' He leaned over and shook out his left leg. 'Now, Moaning Panty Bum, what is it I can help you with?'

The general growled. 'Master Sushi, I am greatly troubled – I am the most mind-blowingly talented rock star and evil supervillain the planet has ever known, yet I have failed to take over the world. Two times I have tried, and two times I have been thwarted by the snivelling pipsqueak Zero Boy. It makes me angry. It makes me *very* angry. Why have I not succeeded? What am I doing wrong?' He stared at the old master. 'Tell me, what is the secret to achieving world domination?'

Master Sushi scratched his chin. 'Hmmm . . . these very difficult questions . . . need time to think of answers.' He clasped his red-freckled hands over his eyes.

'*A-um – a-um – a-um*,' he muttered again.

A few seconds later he reached inside his robe,

pulled out a small crumbly object and placed it in the general's hands.

'Have cupcake,' he smiled.

'What!' the general howled. 'Have a cupcake? Listen, I came here for evil guidance, not a morning tea break!'

'Ssssh,' Master Sushi tapped the general's head. 'Ears work much better when mouth is full.'

The general reluctantly bit into the cupcake.

'Mouldy Pancake Tin . . . you fail for two reasons. First reason is because of your great anger. You must not be angry any more. You must reject anger like child who spits out half-eaten worm they find in old apple.'

The general gulped.

'Second reason you fail is because you seek great fame. Do not seek fame. You must forget big "rock star" image. Be humble and quiet like common fruit fly who is happy living amongst droppings under cherry tree.'

The general almost choked on his cupcake.

The old master took a deep breath. 'You must rid yourself of these terrible desires – and then you will no longer fail.'

'*What!!*' the general bellowed, stomping his foot on the ground. 'Are you out of your muppety mind? I can't change everything that's unbelievably cool, dynamic and hip about me. No way!!! And you know what you can do with your cupcakes!' He stormed off angrily down the mountain.

Ten minutes later he returned, looking rather sheepish.

'Look, old man – perhaps I was a bit hasty back then. How about I cut you a deal? I'll drop the anger, but I'll still hang on to the fame. How's that?'

Master Sushi shook his head. 'Uh-uh. To become my apprentice you must change completely, or you fail.'

'Well then, how about just a few small statues and a fan club?'

The old master frowned and crossed his arms.

The general threw his hands up in disgust. 'Oh,

all right, then ... have it your way. It repulses me, but I'll agree to make a few changes here and there.' He stared at the master. 'But before I do that, tell me – what is the secret to world domination?'

Master Sushi pulled out another cupcake and placed it in the general's hands.

'The answer, apprentice, is in *your* hands.'

The general snarled. 'Oh, come on now, enough with this ninnyish nonsense. I told you, I want answers, not appetisers!'

Master Sushi slowly shook his head. 'No, no ... you not listen. I say the answer you seek is in your hands. *Cupcake* is answer!'

'Huh?' The general inspected the cupcake.

'Cupcake is made from very special ancient recipe. When person eat cupcake, it release chemical that make them lighter. After eating many cupcakes, person float away up into space. Bye-bye, Planet Earth. So, you must feed everyone with cupcake. When they all gone into space, you have whole planet to yourself to do what you like with.'

The general's eyes lit up. 'My word! That's unbelievable!!!'

'One hundred cupcakes enough to make normal person float into space.' The old master grinned evilly. 'And just one cupcake enough to make superhero disappear. Superheroes have powers to become nearly weightless when they want to fly through sky like bird. But nasty cupcake spoil these powers and make them completely weightless and cause them to float away.'

The general jumped for joy and whooped. 'Master Sushi!' he boomed. 'This is an incredible invention.' He shook the cupcake jubilantly above his head. 'I've never heard of something so simple and sinister before. It's pure brilliance.' He patted the old master heartily on the back. 'Listen, you strange little man, you might smell like a wet

hamster's armpit and have the dress sense of a
homeless garden gnome, but when it comes to
being evil, you're an uncontested genius!' He
clapped his hands together and cackled. 'All right,
when do we get started making these cupcakes?'

Master Sushi raised his hand. 'Patience ... first
we must find you a new name.'

'What? A new name? Why?'

'New name prove to everyone you become new
person. No more big General Rock Star.' Master
Sushi leaned back and made a gargling noise in
his throat. He slapped his cheeks hard and quickly

19

stood straight again.

He glanced at the general. 'From now on, the world shall know you as . . . *Snowflake*.'

'S-Snowflake!' the general bellowed, almost tripping over his feet. 'That's ridiculous – you can't call me that. Surely you must be joking?'

Master Sushi shook his head. 'Uh-uh, Master Sushi never joke.' He grinned quietly to himself. 'Although, one time, when Master Sudoku was not looking I put Vaseline on his toilet seat. When he go to use loo, he slip off and fall badly on ground! Very funny joke . . .'

BALLOON BOY'S BOGUS BIRTHDAY BASH

One month later . . .

'Happy birthday to you . . . happy birthday dear
Charlie . . .'

Charlie's eyes bulged as a huge sticky white
cake covered with flaming candles was placed on
the table in front of him.

'Go on, make a wish, Charlie,' Dad cried.

'Huh, I bet you're going to wish for
Commander Ron's latest PlayStation game, eh,'
Josh cheered.

Charlie shook his head. 'Nup, actually I couldn't
think of any better birthday wish than to see

General Pandemonium's ugly face behind bars again!'

Josh laughed.

Charlie closed his eyes. But as he leaned over the cake, the smoke from the candles tickled his nostrils. He felt a throbbing sensation in the back of his nose. 'A . . . A . . . A . . . A-CHOO!!' Charlie exploded with a super sneeze sending the sticky white cake – KER-SPLATT – flying across the room and hitting the back wall.

'Charlie!!!' Mum cried.

Charlie opened his eyes. 'Oops,' he gulped. 'I really *wish* I hadn't just done that.'

Trixie howled in despair. 'Mr Tiddlebinks! Mr Tiddlebinks? Where's Mr Tiddlebinks?' she

shrieked. 'Charlie's blown him away!'

Josh pointed to his left. 'Um, I think that cat-shaped snowman over there licking his paws is who you're looking for.'

'Oh, Mr Tiddlebinks!' Trixie bellowed, rushing to the aid of her beloved moggy covered in sticky whipped cream.

Mum wiped the goo off her face and arms. 'Um, Charlie – that was, er, most unexpected . . .' She scraped the remains of the cake off the wall and composed herself. 'Now – we can't have this little mishap ruining your special day, can we?' She turned and headed towards the kitchen. 'Don't worry – I've got something else delicious we can eat instead.'

A few moments later she returned carrying a tray of scrumptious-looking cupcakes.

'These are the latest craze in health foods – they're called Zero G Cupcakes.

Charlie eyed up the plate and started drooling.

'They're the scrummiest, most divine cupcakes I've ever tasted in my life. And do you know what the most amazing thing of all is about them?'

Charlie shook his head.

'They're so incredibly healthy that, when you eat them, you actually lose weight.'

'Really?' Dad exclaimed.

'Yes,' Mum replied. 'Sylvia at the tennis club lost nearly three kilograms last week just from eating these cupcakes alone!'

Charlie fingered one of the cupcakes. 'What does "Zero G" stand for?' he said, looking at the logo emblazoned on the wrapper.

Mum shrugged her shoulders. 'I don't know – maybe it stands for zero grams or something . . .'

Charlie popped one of the juicy cupcakes into his mouth. 'Mmm . . . awesome . . .' He hummed, licking his lips. 'Mum, this is the yummiest thing

I've ever tasted in my life.'

Mum beamed. 'See, I told you you'd like them.'

She offered the plate to the others. 'C'mon, everybody, help yourselves. Who's going to be next?' Mum glanced over her shoulder. 'Trixie, sweetie, come over and have one or else you'll miss out.'

Trixie turned up her nose. 'Cupcakes are for babies. I don't want to eat baby food at a baby party.' She picked up Mr Tiddlebinks and marched off towards the bathroom to clean him up.

'Ah well, that just means more for us, then,' Dad grinned, eagerly eyeing up the plate.

Charlie rubbed his belly. 'Yummm, I'm going to have another one.' He reached out towards the plate but suddenly his eyes rolled back in his head and – **SWISHH** – he flipped upside down and started floating up towards the ceiling.

'What the—!' he bellowed, looking down at the floor disappearing below him.

'Oh my,' Mum cried, dropping the plate of cupcakes.

'Oi, Charlie . . . what are you doing up there?' Josh shouted.

Mum looked up and frowned. 'Now, Charlie, I know you're excited about the cupcakes, but please don't show off in front of your friend like this. Come back down at once.'

Charlie waved his arms about frantically. 'Mum, I'm not showing off. I'm really stuck up here!'

Dad walked underneath him and scratched his head. 'How bizarre.'

Josh picked a cupcake off the floor and inspected it. 'Hey, Charlie, do you think the cupcake caused this?'

Charlie looked blank. 'I dunno. How could it do that?'

Mum crossed her arms. 'How absurd. Who ever heard of a cupcake causing someone to float up to

THE CURSE OF THE CANTANKEROUS CUPCAKE COSTUME

Meanwhile, on the other side of the city, the world's most deadly supervillain marched through the middle of the town's biggest shopping mall with an angry look on his face. He glared at the passers-by staring at him.

'Cupcakes . . . get your cupcakes here!' he boomed from inside a giant cupcake costume.

A doddery old lady wobbled over towards him. 'Oh, hello dear, aren't you a sight? I've never met a talking cupcake before. Tell me, what's your name?'

The general thrust out a basket of cupcakes into the old lady's face. 'Just take a cupcake and get lost, old lady.'

'Oh – how rude!' The shocked old woman plucked a cupcake out of the basket and waddled away.

The general turned to Master Sushi. 'Do I *really* have to wear this ridiculous costume?' he rasped. 'I just don't see the point of it.'

Master Sushi smiled. 'Yes, Snowflake . . . you must wear costume.' He clasped his hands together. 'Cupcake costume *very* important part of your training.'

The general groaned loudly. 'Hmmm, is that so? I didn't realise that prancing about in public dressed as a total and utter ninny would help me learn how to be a successful "evil" world leader. What else have you got in store for me? Rollerblading backwards wearing a glow-in-the-dark chicken suit?'

Master Sushi cleared his throat. 'Snowflake – cupcake costume teach you valuable lesson about being humble team player. To be great evil leader – you must first be great evil servant. Your crew are busy at factory baking cupcakes, and now you too are busy making people eat the cupcakes. You become a team player now. You are like hard-working ant helping other hard-working ants.'

The general scowled. 'I wish you were an ant, then I'd squash you.'

Feeling breathless, the general stopped and bent over, resting his hands on his knees.

'Argh, I'm dying of thirst in here – this costume is like a sauna.'

Just then a red-headed schoolboy ran up behind him and kicked him in the backside.

'Ha-ha, take that, muffin-head!' the schoolboy cackled as he sprinted off.

'Wha—!!!' The general sprung back up and shook his fist wildly. 'Come here, you little

scumbag . . . !'

Master Sushi grabbed his arm. 'Uh–uh . . . Snowflake, no, do not be violent. You must not harm schoolboy, especially ginger one.'

He placed his hands either side of the general's big plastic cupcake head. 'Listen, Snowflake – I now teach very important lesson about anger.' He cleared his throat and stared into the general's eyes.

'Anger is *very* bad thing. Anger lead to frustration . . . frustration lead to hatred . . . and hatred lead to . . .' Master Sushi suddenly paused.

'Yes, yes . . .' The general grunted. 'Hatred leads to what?'

Master Sushi rubbed his forehead. 'Oops, ah, Master Sushi forget last line of important saying.'

'What?' The general snapped. 'You're supposed to be the wisest evil mind in the entire galaxy! Surely you've memorised all this stuff by now?'

Master Sushi shook his head. 'Yes, but last week Master Sushi go on special retraining course. Now we have new popular saying. Master Sushi so used to old words, very hard to remember new words.'

Josh quickly pulled his arm down.
'No, no, wait, it's too early for you
to start flying again. You weren't
much good at it to begin with, and
being weightless might have stuffed
up your sense of balance.'

Charlie brushed Josh's hand away.
'Don't worry – I'll be fine, honestly.'
He puffed out his chest. 'Hero Boy
to the rescue!' **WOOSH** – he blasted
off the ground but – **THONG** – he
immediately smashed head-first into a
lamppost, then – **BOING** – rebounded
into the middle of the tree – **KERRACK**
– snapping it in half. 'Arghh!!!' Charlie
plummeted to the ground holding the broken
top half of the tree above his head with Mr
Tiddlebinks trapped inside it. **KERTHUD** – he
slammed down hard onto the pavement
and – **KERRROWWWW** – Mr Tiddlebinks
flopped down on top of his face, digging
his claws hard into Charlie's nose.

'Yeoww!!!' Charlie screamed as

the hissing cat leapt off his face and scurried away.

Josh jogged over. 'Hey, Charlie, are you okay? That looked really nasty.'

Charlie rubbed his nose. 'Ow, I think that's going to leave a mark.'

Josh helped him back to his feet. 'Okay, well, at least we know that your flying powers are totally back to normal again!'

Josh and Charlie jogged slowly back across the street.

Just then – **SCREECH** – Dad pulled into the driveway with Trixie sitting in the front seat. He hopped out with a huge beaming smile on his face, not noticing the broken tree lying on the other side of the street.

'Charlie – oh my word – you're back to your old self again. Hooray!' He chortled. 'Dr Hamill's medicine worked!!!'

Charlie smiled. 'Um, well, not exactly . . .'

'C'mon let's go inside and celebrate,' Dad giggled, grabbing Charlie's arm.

Josh bent over at the knees, still gasping for fresh air. 'Ah – somehow I don't think that's going to happen.'

Charlie skipped over to his mum and hugged her. 'I'm cured – I'm cured,' he beamed. 'Mum – I'm not going to spend the rest of my life as a balloon!'

'That's nice, dear,' Mum said, smiling politely.

Josh stood up and looked over at them. 'Hey, Mrs A, I bet you're super relieved to have Charlie back to normal again, eh!'

Mum wiped her brow. 'Absolutely . . . I couldn't cope with one day more of Charlie's dreadful boots leaving marks on our lovely new carpet!'

DEAR OH DEAR, DAD

A few seconds later, Mum marched off and started manically spraying inside the house with a super-strength air-freshener.

Josh let out a loud cough. 'Charlie . . . I think you've just discovered your most deadly superpower yet!'

Charlie groaned. 'Tell me about it. I'm never going to eat another baked bean again in my life. It's just lucky nobody got injured during the explosions.'

'Speak for yourself,' Josh said, pointing across the street. 'You blew your sister's cat up into that tree over there!'

Charlie gulped loudly. 'Oh, no . . . Trixie's going to kill me. I'd better fly up there and rescue Mr Tiddlebinks right now before I'm dead meat.' He thrust his fist into the air.

Charlie shrugged his shoulders. 'I'm not sure. Dr Hamill said there might be some really nasty bugs going around at the moment. Mum reckons I got it because I haven't been washing my hands carefully enough after playing outside.'

Josh stared at Charlie's boots.

'But what about the cupcake! Did you tell your doctor about the cupcake you ate yesterday?'

Charlie shook his head. 'Nah, I was going to tell him, but he had to rush off for an important game of golf.'

'Oh, this is nuts,' Josh moaned. 'So, when are you going to be back to normal again?'

'I dunno . . . Dr Hamill doesn't really know either.' Charlie held up a small white bottle. 'But he gave me some medicine to take – maybe that might help me get better.'

Josh scratched his head. 'So, are you allowed to go outside?'

Charlie smiled. 'Of course – I just have to be really careful if it gets windy.' He glanced at his watch. 'Hey, did you hear that Commander Ron and the Terrific Twelve are going to be at the opening of the new Mega Sports Stadium this morning? Shall we go down and check them out?'

Josh paused for a moment. 'Um, yeah, sure . . . but how do you plan to walk all the way to the stadium in those gigantic clod-hoppers?'

Charlie grinned. 'Very noisily . . .'

Half an hour later, Charlie and Josh arrived at the Mega Sports Stadium. They joined the back of a large noisy crowd waiting expectantly to see the superheroes.

'Hey, I can see them,' Charlie cheered, peering up into the sky with his super vision.

DA-DA-DA-DA-DA! Trumpets sounded and dozens of muscular superheroes descended triumphantly from the clouds.

'Awesome – hey, look, there's Commander Ron,' Charlie said, waving frantically.

Josh's face lit up. 'I wonder what show they're going to put on for us today. Maybe they'll do a supersonic acrobatic display . . . or maybe Commander Ron will try and lift fifty tanks

shorts, rattling the foundations of the house and
setting off all the smoke alarms.

'Uarghh . . .' Josh clutched his throat and
desperately crawled outside.

Mum ran inside from the garden. 'Ohh . . .
my word!' she shrieked, covering her nose and
immediately running back outside again. 'Help!!!
Help!!!' she hollered. 'There's a gas leak – call the
fire brigade!'

Josh slowly crawled across the grass towards
her. 'No, no, Mrs A – there's no gas leak. It's just
Charlie – he's got really bad wind.'

Just then Charlie stumbled out the
front door and collapsed to his knees.

PHARRRRRRRRRPPPPP!!! Another thundering explosion rattled out of his backside, blasting a surprised Mr Tiddlebinks high up into the air.

Charlie turned bright red. 'Er, sorry about that, Mum . . . it was the beans!'

Mum put her hands on her hips. 'Charlie Applejack, how many times have I told you – never eat baked beans. You know what havoc they cause with your digestive system.'

'I know, Mum, but I had to . . .' Charlie groaned. 'Josh was trying to find a cure for me!'

'A cure for what? What are you talking about?'

Josh staggered over to Charlie. 'Hey, mate, did it work?' he puffed. 'Are you fixed yet?'

Charlie slowly stood up. 'I dunno.' He gingerly pulled his left lead boot off, then a few seconds later, his right one. He stretched out his toes and dug his heels solidly into the grass. 'Whoo-hoo! I think I'm cured!' He jumped up and down normally on the spot. He gave Josh a high five. 'Josh, you're a genius – you should win the Nobel prize for discovering this cure.'

as a balloon.' He grimaced. 'But don't stick any
needles into me – and I'm not going to have an
operation!'

Josh smiled. 'Don't worry – we don't need
to stick needles in you or make you have an
operation. I've got a
much easier way to
make your body get
rid of the gas.'

'What's that?' Charlie cried.

Josh grinned. 'Baked beans!'

One hour later . . .

Charlie and Josh sat at the kitchen table. Charlie's
eyes were bulging like lemons.

'C'mon, Charlie, just one more can should do it,'
Josh urged.

Charlie groaned. 'Are you serious? I've already eaten three cans – I think I'm going to be sick! I don't even like the taste of baked beans.'

Josh shoved the can in front of him. 'C'mon, Charlie – do it for the missing superheroes. Do it for the fate of mankind.'

'Arghhh,' Charlie reluctantly shovelled another spoonful of lumpy cold beans into his trembling mouth.

Suddenly he dropped his spoon on the table.

'What's wrong?' Josh cried.

Charlie gripped his rumbling belly. 'R–run . . . quick . . . run!!!'

But before Josh could make it out of the room Charlie doubled over and – **PHARRRRRRRRRPPPPP** – blasted a volcanic-like eruption out of the back of his shorts. **KERWHOOSH** – Josh was sent flying across the room, landing – **KERFLOP** – in a pile of towels in the laundry.

Charlie clutched his throbbing tummy again. **PHARRRRRRRRRPPPPP!!!** An even more powerful explosion thundered out of his

He rustled about in his pocket. 'Ah, here are my notes from training course.'

He stared at the general again. 'I say . . . anger lead to frustration . . . frustration lead to hatred . . . and hatred lead to . . . *happy customers*.'

'Happy customers?' the general howled. 'What on earth are you going on about, you geriatric old goon!'

Master Sushi turned bright red. 'Oops, look like Master Sushi have notes from wrong training course.' He wiped his brow. 'Ah, perhaps time now for Master Sushi to have a little break. Brain work much better with hot drink inside body.' He stuffed the notes back into his pocket and ambled off

towards a nearby coffee shop.

The general groaned. '*You* need a break! Huh. Why don't you try lugging this giant costume around all day, to see what feeling tired is like!' He waved at the old master. 'Oi, while you're in there, get me a drink too, will you. A cold one. It's hotter than the Sahara desert inside this ridiculous thing!'

Master Sushi turned and shook his head. 'Sorry – only master may drink now. You must wait.'

The general stomped his foot angrily. 'What? Oh – I get it, this is another one of your silly mind games, isn't it? See how long poor Snowflake can last without water, just so he can learn some valuable new lesson . . .'

Master Sushi shrugged his shoulders. 'No – I only have one coupon for a free drink today. I must have dropped your coupon on the street back there somewhere. Sorry . . .'

TA-TA, TERRIFIC TWELVE

Early the following morning . . .

Josh knocked loudly on the Applejacks' front door. Charlie's mum opened it.

'Hi, Mrs A, is Charlie feeling better today?' Josh asked.

Mum looked over her shoulder. 'Um, judge for yourself.'

CLOMP CLOMP CLOMP CLOMP.

Charlie pounded noisily down the hallway wearing a pair of giant lead boots.

Josh's eyebrows arched. 'Charlie, what on earth have you got on your feet?'

Charlie lifted his leg up. 'Deep-sea diving boots.

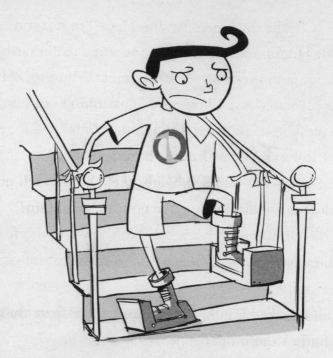

They're super heavy – they keep me from floating off the ground. Dr Hamill borrowed them from the navy museum.'

Josh gulped. 'Huh – what's wrong with you?'

'Dr Hamill said I've got gravititis. He said my body is no longer affected by gravity!'

'Gravititis!' Josh barked. 'I've never heard of that before. It sounds ridiculous. How do you catch gravititis?'

item. Commander Ron signed it for me at his latest book launch.' Charlie pulled the balloon down from the ceiling by its string. 'It's filled with super-helium – Commander Ron said it can float higher and last longer than any other balloon in the world.'

'Cool.' Josh punched the balloon, sending it floating back up in the air again. **BOING** – it bobbed back and forth underneath the ceiling. Suddenly his eyes lit up. 'Hey, Charlie, I think I've just figured out the answer to your problem!'

'You've what?' Charlie gulped.

Josh pulled the balloon back down again. 'Listen, what keeps Commander Ron's balloon afloat?'

Charlie pursed his lips. 'Um . . . the super helium . . .'

'Yep . . .' Josh squeezed the neck of the balloon tight. 'And what happens if the helium gets out of the balloon?'

'Um, it doesn't float any more.'

'Exactly!' Josh quickly undid the string around the balloon's neck and let it go. **PZRRRPPPPPPPPPPPPP**!!!

The balloon manically rocketed around the room, whizzing past Charlie's head before collapsing in a hissing heap on the floor.

'Oi,' Charlie bellowed. 'You've ruined my best balloon!'

Josh smiled. 'Charlie – that's it – don't you see? You're just like a balloon too. Your body must have some evil gas inside it to keep you floating up in the air!'

'I'm filled with evil gas?' Charlie barked.

'Well, sort of – the cupcake must have some chemical ingredient in it that creates something like a gas inside your body!'

Charlie gripped his belly. 'Oh, this is bad.'

Josh nodded. 'I know.'

Charlie stared at Josh. 'We've got to get this evil gas out of my body, and we've got to get it out right now! I don't want to live the rest of my life

THE BALLISTIC BAKED-BEAN BREEZE

An hour later, Charlie and Josh returned to the Applejack household.

Charlie pointed at the clouds above. 'This is a disaster,' he growled. 'Commander Ron and the Terrific Twelve have just disappeared and nobody is even slightly worried about it!'

Josh frowned. 'I know, but that's because nobody understands that the cupcakes are *evil* like we do.' He kicked a stone across the lawn. 'Hey, Charlie – how come normal people aren't disappearing yet as well? Why is it just superheroes?'

Charlie shrugged his shoulders. 'I dunno. Maybe the cupcake's effects work faster on superheroes.

We must be more sensitive to them. If you think about it, our bodies become almost weightless when we hover and fly. The cupcakes must be making us uncontrollably weightless!'

'Maybe . . .'

Josh ran in through the front door and then skipped up the stairs to Charlie's bedroom. 'C'mon – we've gotta find out who's behind the evil cupcakes and take them down big time!'

'I know, I know,' Charlie replied, clomping noisily behind him. 'But first we have to find a cure for my weightlessness. There's no way I can take the bad guys down if I'm floating off the ground all the time.'

Josh slumped down at Charlie's desk. 'Maybe there's some information about a cure on the internet?' He pressed the power button on the computer and waited for it to boot up. While he was sitting there, he noticed a brightly coloured balloon bobbing above him on the ceiling.

'Hey, Charlie . . . is that an official Commander Ron balloon?'

Charlie nodded. 'Yep, it's a special collector's

Suddenly Master Sushi clapped his hands together and ran over. 'No, Snowflake. Stop your talk now! No more talk about fame. No more talk about rock star!'

He grabbed the iPad out of the lieutenant's hands and glared at the screen. 'Rock music – very bad. Dancing prisoners – very bad. Fame on internet – very bad.' He paused for a minute. 'Hoi – but moonwalk . . . hmmm this look *very* cool . . . I must learn sometime.'

The old master tucked the iPad under his arm. 'Do you understand what I'm saying, Snowflake? Are you going to obey my commands?'

The fuming general clenched his fists together. 'Arghh . . . yes . . . yes, of course,' he grizzled, heading off towards the door.

'Where are you going now?' Master Sushi asked.

'Well, if you must know, you nosy little ninny, I'm feeling a bit stressed, so I'm going out for a massage and a long dip in a hot pool.'

Master Sushi shook his head. 'Uh-uh. No massage for you today.' He pointed at a white coat and a plastic hair protector hanging on a hook. 'Now is your turn to put on cooking uniform and help rest of crew bake more cupcakes.'

'Me – bake cupcakes?' The general stuttered. 'Surely you can't be serious!'

The old master grinned. 'You should know by now that Master Sushi *always* serious.' He chuckled quietly under his breath. 'Now, quickly, put on silly pointy hat and go get baking.'

humble beginnings. If you continue to be humble then you will have great success. But if you do not listen to my advice – you will fail.'

'Yes, yes, yes . . . whatever,' the general said, walking off.

Just then, Lieutenant Kurse entered the staff room.

'Ah, General Snowball, sir!'

The general shook his fist. 'Listen, my new name's Snowflake, you nincompoop. Don't you read your e-mails?'

'Er, my apologies, General Snowman . . .'

'I said SNOWFLAKE, you moron!!!'

'Oh, yes, yes, right, right. Sorry, sir, I must have, ah, er, blocked ears today.'

'Now, what is it, Lieutenant?' The general barked.

'Sir, amazing news! Check out this new video.' The lieutenant held up an iPad in front of the general's face. 'Some prisoners in a Seychelles jail have filmed themselves dancing to your song "Stop, Drop and Grovel". Look, they're copying all your dance moves from your music video as well,

even the moonwalk!'

The general's face lit up.

'Sir, this video is spreading across the internet like wildfire. Nearly fifty million people have downloaded it already this morning. That's mind-blowing! The press are going absolutely bonkers over it. Every music journalist in the world wants to speak with you right now.'

The general puffed out his chest and preened his moustache. 'Well, Lieutenant, what can I say? I was born to *rock* and I was born to *rule*!'

jeered. 'My grandmother could eat more cupcakes than you lot put together!'

Josh watched in horror as the superheroes disappeared helplessly into the clouds.

Charlie ran his hands through his hair. 'Josh, I think I've figured out what Zero G stands for.'

'What?'

'Zero Gravity!!!'

BiG, BAD AND BAKiNG MAD

Deep in the heart of the Zero G cupcake factory,
a huge **HOORAY!** went up as the general and his
crew watched the superheroes disappearing live on
TV in the staff room.

'Oh goody!' the general bellowed, leaping up
out of his seat. 'Look at them floating away –
every single stinking one of them!' He punched
the air with delight. 'Master Sushi, you're a genius.
These catastrophic cupcakes are the most brilliant
evil invention ever – and the best thing of all
about them is, no one suspects they're even slightly
sinister!'

Master Sushi nodded quietly. 'See, Snowflake,
like I always tell you, all great ideas come from

above his head!'

Just then giant video screens flickered into life and ten-metre-tall live images of the mighty superheroes beamed out in front of the crowd.

Charlie pointed at one of the screens. 'Huh? Someone's putting some bibs around their necks.'

'Bibs?' Josh cried. 'What are the bibs for?'

Charlie stared closely at the screen. 'Hey, it looks like they're going to have a super-eating competition.'

Josh clapped his hands. 'Cool – I bet Garbo Boy wins this one easily. I hear he can swallow a nuclear bomb and not even get a tummy ache!'

A group of chefs wearing tall white hats marched out towards the superheroes carrying large silver dining trays. They placed the trays in front of the contestants, then slowly removed their lids.

Charlie did a double-take. 'Hey, look – they're making them eat cupcakes!'

Josh's face dropped. 'Charlie – those are just like the one you ate. Look, look – they have that weird Zero G logo on them.'

39

Charlie gulped loudly. 'Hey, Josh, I've got a bad feeling about this.'

Josh tugged his arm. 'Well do something! Stop them from eating the cupcakes. They might be dangerous for their health!'

Charlie groaned. 'But I can't do anything. Not wearing these stupid boots!'

Suddenly – **BANG!** – a starter gun fired and the superheroes started tucking into the cupcakes.

'*Hooray!!!*' The crowd cheered wildly.

'Oh, no, I can't watch,' Josh said, covering his face.

The superheroes munched away frantically on the cupcakes, then all of a sudden stopped eating and looked at each other with puzzled expressions on their faces. One by one they flipped upside down and started floating up off the ground.

'Oh no . . . it's happening to them too!!!' Charlie moaned.

The crowd started roaring with disapproval.

'Boo.'

'Hiss.'

'Wimps.'

'Oi, keep eating,' the man in front of Charlie

Inside the kitchen Dad opened a large cardboard box. 'Dig in; don't wait,' he boomed. 'Let's all have a cupcake to celebrate Charlie returning to normal again!'

'What!!' Charlie bellowed.

'C'mon, I've just brought some juicy vanilla-tang-flavoured cupcakes from the supermarket. Mmmm, they taste delicious.'

Charlie threw his arms up in the air. 'Dad, what are you doing?' he howled. 'Don't you know those things are deadly?'

Dad smiled and popped a cupcake into his mouth. 'Charlie, what on earth are you talking about? These little gems are brilliant. They're the sole reason I weigh the same now as I did when I was a teenager ...'

Mum walked into the kitchen 'Oh, great, you've got some more cupcakes. I was going to do a workout at the gym tonight, but now I'll just pop a couple of these beauties down and that should knock off a kilo or two instead.'

Charlie's face screwed up. 'Mum, Dad, you are out of your minds. Those things cause you to float off the ground!'

Mum laughed. 'Oh, Charlie – what a load of nonsense. You've been reading too many of those wacky stories on the internet again, haven't you?'

Dad wiped his mouth. 'Charlie, these cupcakes are potentially the greatest health-food invention since low-calorie milk or even sugar-free chocolate.'

Charlie groaned.

'In fact, I love these cupcakes so much that I've volunteered to give a free motivational speech to the staff and management at Zero G cupcakes. I want to help them make their product an even bigger global success!'

Charlie groaned again and rolled his eyes.

Josh leaned over and quietly whispered in his ear. 'Um, I don't mean to be a whiner, but do you think your parents could be any more unhelpful towards our mission to save the world?'

BING BONG*. You have reached your destination.*
A soft voice echoed from the GPS system on the
dashboard.

Dad smiled and pulled into the VIP visitor's
parking spot. He gathered up his speaking notes
and opened the door.

'All righty,' he said chirpily. 'It's time to brighten,
enlighten, and start getting excitin'.'

CAUGHT ON CANDID CUPCAKE CAMERA

A small, frail man hobbled out of the main entrance to welcome Dad.

'Ah, greetings Mr Jack Apple, welcome . . . I am Master Sushi.'

Dad smiled and shook the old man's hand. 'Great to meet you, sir — but if you don't mind, my name's actually Mr Applejack.'

Master Sushi looked blank. 'Whatever . . .' He then clasped his hands together. 'Mr Jack, I must thank you for writing your famous book, *If You Blink — Then You Can Think*. It truly changed my life.'

'Oh, really?' Dad said, puffing his chest out.

'Yes!' The old master beamed. 'Many moons

Come Home Princess Daddy Wuvs You Vewy Much

a roundabout and then sped down a long tree-lined road. As they drove along, Charlie and Josh noticed a series of strange poodle-shaped signs in the grass by the side of the road.

Charlie squinted. 'Huh? "Missing Poodle –

Reward Five Million Pounds". What the . . .?'

'"Help me rescue my dog".' Josh read. '"Call 0800-Find-Miffy-Wiffy"?'

Just then a plane flew overhead towing a bright red banner behind

it on which was printed *Come Home Princess – Daddy Wuvs You Vewy Vewy Much.*

Charlie scratched his head. 'This is bizarre.' He craned his neck looking up at the plane flying overhead. 'Who goes to all this trouble over some stupid dog?'

Josh looked puzzled.

Charlie slumped back

in his seat. 'I mean . . . five million pounds for a poodle — that's bonkers.' Suddenly an ice-cold chill raced down his spine. His mouth dropped wide open. 'Oh, no . . . no, please . . . no.'

Josh stared at Charlie. 'What's wrong?'

Charlie cupped his face in his hands. 'Josh, what maniac do we know who is that much into poodles?'

Josh moaned loudly. 'No, Charlie, please say it isn't so . . .'

Charlie nodded. 'Yep. There's only one freak show in this world would go to that much trouble over a poodle — *General Pandemonium.*'

Josh thumped his seat. 'Ohh . . . this sucks. It's so typical. Those evil cupcakes are his idea, aren't they? He wants every human on earth to float away so he can have the entire planet all to himself!'

'Yep.' Charlie bent down and zipped up his sports bag with his superhero costume hidden inside it. 'But don't worry, Josh; we're going to stop that big-nosed bird-brained loser before he gets even close to doing it!'

THE MISERY OF THE MISSING MUTT

Ten minutes later, Dad's station wagon was driving down the motorway with Trixie in the front seat and Charlie and Josh sitting quietly in the back.

'Psst . . . Charlie,' Josh whispered. 'What did you have to bribe your sister with to make her come along?'

Charlie sighed heavily. 'Ugh, it was ugly – I promised her she could use my PSP whenever she wanted to – even if I was in the middle of a high-score game, and I also promised her I'd do all her dishwashing and cleaning chores for the next two months as well.'

Josh grimaced. 'Ouch, you're right – that's

ugly.' He glanced out the window then looked at his watch. 'Excuse me, Mr Applejack, but do you know how long it will take us to get to the Zero G cupcake factory?'

Dad looked up in the rear-view mirror. 'Hmmmm, interesting question, Josh. Let me answer your question with another question – which do you think is more important, the *time* the journey takes, or the *times* you experience on the journey?'

Josh went blank. 'Huh?'

Charlie leaned forward and stared at the 'time-remaining' display on the GPS screen in the middle of the dashboard. 'Ignore him, Josh – we'll be there in fifteen minutes.'

Josh smiled. 'Cool.'

Fourteen minutes later, Dad pulled off the motorway and headed towards a long bridge. Charlie peered ahead into the distance. 'That must be the cupcake factory over there,' he said pointing to a massive complex to the right of them.

Dad crossed over the bridge, turned right at

Just then Dad skipped down the stairs with a beaming smile on his face. 'Hey, everybody – I just got a call from Zero G cupcakes,' he whooped. 'They've taken me up on my offer. They want me to drop everything and come over to their factory right away. I'm going to give a big speech about teamwork to their staff before they undertake a new massive global takeover operation!'

Josh slapped Charlie on the back. 'I feel a plan coming together . . .'

Charlie raced over to Dad. 'Dad, Dad, wait up a minute. I've always wanted to hear one of your awesome speeches. Can I come along too?'

Dad did a double-take. 'You want to hear me speak today? At the Zero G cupcake factory?'

'Sure . . . it'll be cool. Can Josh come too?'

Dad giggled. 'Absolutely – the more the merrier.' He glanced at his watch. 'Oh, there's just one problem, though – we can't leave Trixie home by herself. Mum's out playing tennis at the moment.'

'Um, maybe she could come too,' Charlie said scratching his chin.

Dad sighed. 'Ahh, I don't think so . . . *Alien Pet Swap*, her favourite TV programme, is on this afternoon, and you know how cranky she gets if she misses it.'

Charlie smiled. 'Don't worry, Dad, leave it to me – I'll take care of it.'

'Huh, what's happening?' Charlie cried.

Josh pointed at the screen. 'Remember those overweight pop stars who went to Chubba Chubba Island last week on that TV game show?'

Charlie nodded.

'Well, they've all disappeared! Every single one of them.' Josh turned up the volume. 'All they had to eat on the island was an unlimited supply of Zero G cupcakes. They were competing to see who could lose the most weight.'

The reporter's ruddy face filled the screen. 'That's right, Lindsay. Tragically, twenty-five of

our most beloved portly pop stars have apparently vanished into thin air, if you'll pardon the pun. Legendary performers such as Lady Choc Bar, Puffed-Up Daddy and Take Fat are missing without a trace. Authorities fear it could be the work of pirates, or, worse still — perhaps the pop stars may have been mistaken for a pod of small whales while swimming, and eaten by killer sharks.'

Charlie turned off the TV and grunted. 'Huh, they haven't been eaten by killer sharks, they're floating up into the clouds like runaway blimps.' He clasped his hands over his face. 'Oh, Josh, this is seriously bad news.'

'I know,' Josh groaned. 'My mum is a huge Lady Choc Bar fan.'

Charlie looked at the clock on the wall and sighed loudly. 'Josh, we're running out of time — normal people are disappearing too! We have to act — and we have to act right now!'

Josh jumped to his feet. 'But Charlie, we don't have a plan! We don't even know who's making the cupcakes or where they're located.'

The old master lifted the rice paper closer to his face. Suddenly his eyes bulged and his mouth dropped wide open as he read – '*Splat – I squash butterfly in my wide-open hands and flick him away like old snot . . .*' He ripped up the haiku and stomped on it angrily. 'Bad!! Bad!! Bad!!' he roared. 'Very bad, Snowflake – you do not kill people in a haiku!'

'Argghhh!!' The general leapt out of his chair and lunged at the lieutenant's throat.

Lieutenant Kurse quickly ducked to his left, spun around and rapidly back-pedalled out of the office.

'I'll come back when the general's calmed down!' he shouted.

Master Sushi followed him out the door and called after him. 'What time I tell Snowflake you return?'

'Sometime next century!' the lieutenant wailed, disappearing down the hallway.

THE CURIOUS CASE OF THE CHUBBA CHUBBA CATASTROPHE

Back at the Applejacks', Charlie urgently scanned the internet looking for any background information he could find about Zero G cupcakes, while down in the lounge Josh sat glued to the TV, watching a late-breaking news item.

'Charlie, Charlie!' he bellowed. 'Quick – come and check this out!'

Charlie scuttled down the stairs and raced into the lounge.

'And now . . .' the newsreader buzzed in low tones, 'we take you live to the scene of the mysterious disappearance. This report from Danny Toopay . . .'

THE PETRIFYING POODLE PREDICAMENT

Two hours later . . .

Lieutenant Kurse walked into the general's softly lit office and knocked gently on the carpet-panelled wall.

'Ah, excuse me, er, General Snowcone, I'm sorry to interrupt, but I have some fantastic news for you – we've just sold our ten billionth cupcake. Isn't that staggering? Nearly every man, woman and child on the planet has tasted one of our cupcakes by now.' The lieutenant beamed. 'It won't be long before the entire human race will be floating up into space, sir.'

The general stared blankly at the lieutenant.

Lieutenant Kurse shuffled his feet awkwardly. 'Um, sir, did I say something wrong just then? You don't seem terribly happy about the mind-blowing news.'

The general remained silent.

Master Sushi raised his hand. 'Ah, Snowflake is not allowed to speak right now. This is his final training challenge. He must take vow of silence for one day. If he is successful, then he is ready to be in charge of earth and all its resources.'

The lieutenant paused. 'I'm sorry, but did you say the general is not allowed to speak at all?'

The old master nodded.

'And he's not allowed to say a single thing in response to whatever I say to him?'

The master nodded again. 'No. Not even peep.' He clasped his hands together. 'Snowflake may only communicate by writing little poem. No words may pass through his lips today.'

'Hmmm, most interesting.' Lieutenant Kurse adjusted his top button. 'Well actually, sir, there is this one other little bit of urgent news that I just remembered right now that I have to tell you . . .'

The general reluctantly slumped back in his seat.

The old master quickly handed him another pen. 'Now, is time for you to write poem. Write lieutenant a haiku and tell him what you think of his news.'

The lieutenant scratched his head. 'A what? I'm sorry, did I hear you correctly? Do you want the general to go *hiking*?'

'No.' Master Sushi cried. 'Haiku is ancient type of small poem. I train Snowflake how to write haiku. He use haiku to better express his feelings of anger. No more nasty shouting or bashing. Just clear, calm words instead in haiku.'

'Oh, really?'

The scowling general reluctantly gripped the pen and began scribbling on some rice paper.

'Remember calm, clear words . . .' Master Sushi whispered.

When the snarling general was finished, he put his pen down and handed his haiku to the old man.

Master Sushi briefly glanced at the rice paper. 'Hmmm, very good, I now read aloud.' He cleared his throat.

'*Butterfly float down and tell me news about "fluffy cloud" in the sky.*'

He turned to the lieutenant. 'Ah, you see, in his poem, the butterfly is you – the messenger – and fluffy cloud is his poodle. He say messenger come to tell him news of his dog stuck in the sky. Very good . . . clear, calm words.' He continued reading.

'*Butterfly's news make my eyes open wide, my hands too.*'

The master looked at the lieutenant again. 'Ah, Snowflake is now saying that your news of his dog goes straight into his mind and straight into his heart. His eyes are wide with shock. He spreads his hands as if to say, "Why must this happen?" It upsets him greatly.'

Master Sushi smiled. 'Go ahead . . . tell Snowflake.'

'Um, sir, it concerns your poodle Miffy Wiffy . . .'

The general's eyes fixed on the nervous lieutenant.

'Ah, um, earlier this morning, our scientists reported some rather unfortunate news. Apparently Miffy Wiffy broke into their lab last night and polished off ten boxes of their new bite-sized mini Zero G cupcakes . . .'

The general picked up a pen and gripped it tightly.

'Ah, sir, there's no easy way to say this, but it appears that Miffy Wiffy has now, er, disappeared up into the sky.'

'Aummmmm . . .' the general moaned painfully under his breath.

'But, the news isn't all bad. Luckily, Miffy Wiffy's wearing a GPS collar and we can track exactly where she is.' The lieutenant pulled out a small beeping hand-held screen from his pocket. 'Right now she's about ten kilometres off the ground and drifting across Russia.'

KERRRACK!!! The general snapped the pen in two.

The lieutenant felt a bead of sweat trickle down the back of his neck. 'Now, our radar operators are confident that if the wind changes direction in the next twelve hours, there's a good chance that she might blow back this way again!'

'Aaauuummmm . . .' The general leapt out of his seat and started manically head-butting the filing cabinet. **KERBANGG KERBANGG!**

Master Sushi grabbed him and pulled him away. 'No! Snowflake. Do not use head like hammer. Very bad for brain.'

to speak, go through that orange door over there at end of room – it leads out onto stage.' He pointed at row of TV monitors positioned on the wall. 'Small helpers – you stay here and watch Mr Jack speak on TV. We have many different angles for you to watch.' He passed over a remote. 'And we have digital surround sound too. Very nice for ears.'

Master Sushi bowed. 'I must go and take my seat now.' He waved at Dad. 'Once again, Mr Jack, it is great honour to meet you.'

'Why, you're too kind,' Dad grinned.

After the old master had closed the big blue door, Charlie walked past the plate of cupcakes

and turned his nose up. 'Yecchh, I'm not touching those horrible things.'

Dad checked his teeth in the mirror, picked up his speaking notes and then headed towards the orange door at the end of the room. 'Oh, don't bother about wishing me good luck out there,' he whistled. 'Luck is only for people who don't have clever ideas, well-crafted jokes and sensational hairstyles . . .'

KERCLICK. He shut the door behind him.

As soon as he'd left, Josh and Charlie rushed over to the TV monitors.

'Okay, can you see the general?' Josh said urgently.

Charlie checked the first screen. 'Nup, not on this one.' He jumped over to the next screen. 'Not on this one either.'

Josh raced to the very end screen. His eyes instantly lit up. 'Bingo – I found him!'

THE SINISTER
SNOWFLAKE SECRET

'All right, scumbag, this time I'm taking you down,' Charlie rasped at the screen.

Trixie burst out laughing. 'Huh, listen to you ... you really think you're some big-shot superhero, don't you.'

Charlie glared at his sister. 'Do you mind, I'm on an important mission to save the world here!' He unzipped his sports bag, pulled out his costume and began putting it on.

'You call that a costume?' Trixie snorted. 'So who are you – The Mighty Geek? And what about your sidekick, is he Nerdy Boy?'

Josh grimaced. 'Charlie, is she like this all the time at home?'

Charlie slipped on his dishwashing gloves and swimming cap. 'Nup,' he said, fastening his goggles tight. 'She's being really nice today.'

Charlie rushed back to the TV again.

Josh tapped the screen. 'This is kinda weird; I'd have thought a big shot like the general would be sitting right in the middle of the front row. I don't know why he's located right at the back of the auditorium.'

Charlie peered at the image. 'Hey – am I seeing correctly? Is he serving coffee to those henchmen over there? No way! Surely the galaxy's most deadly maniac isn't in charge of refreshments?'

'Look – what's that sticker on his chest?' Josh whispered.

Charlie zoomed in on the screen with his super-vision. 'Ah, it says . . . "Introducing Snowflake".'

'*Snowflake?* What's that supposed to mean?' Josh quizzed.

Charlie frowned. 'I dunno, but I bet it's something really sinister. Maybe it's a code word for "Super Nuclear Oversized Weapon, Fully Loaded And Killing Everyone" . . . or something mega-dangerous like that.'

'Hmm, catchy name,' said Josh.

Just then Lieutenant Kurse appeared on the screen. He leaned close to the general's ear. The general started throttling him violently, then looked up at the screen and angrily shook his fist.

'Huh?' Josh gulped. 'Is he shaking his fist at us? Can he see us from down there?'

Charlie gasped. 'Oh no, look!' All the TV screens suddenly filled with the image of Charlie and Josh's startled faces. 'We're on TV too!'

Josh looked up and froze. 'Charlie, they've got security cameras filming us – they must have

85

recognised your superhero costume.'

WRONGGG WRONGG. A soft pulsing alarm started flashing above them in the ceiling.

'Oh, no,' Charlie moaned. 'The general's on to us!'

ago I work in boring job at car wash. All day long wash and wax – my brain turn mushier than my sponge. But one day I read a few words from your great book and then decide to quit dull job and go and live on desert island in small hut made of bubblegum. After five years of studying your chapter "Ten easy steps to becoming a genius", I become a genius too. Very amazing!'

Dad grinned from ear to ear. 'Well, what can I say? When I hear that someone quits their job and spends five years living on a desert island in a hut made of bubblegum, just to read one of my books, then I know I've done my job as an author.'

Master Sushi bowed quietly. 'Come now, my team gather in auditorium to hear your great words of inspiration. And, please, bring your small helpers with you too.'

Trixie turned and scowled at Charlie as they walked off. 'No way. I'm not going inside that stupid building. I want to go home, and I want to go now.'

Charlie winced. 'But Trixie, we had a deal, remember!'

Trixie glared at Charlie. 'The deal has changed. If you want me to stay then you'll have to do all my cleaning chores until Christmas now.'

Charlie's eyes bulged. 'Christmas!' He took in a deep breath. 'O-o-kay . . .' he sighed miserably.

Master Sushi led Dad, Trixie, Charlie and Josh through the maze-like building until they reached a waiting room adjoining the main auditorium.

'Mr Jack, this is your place to rest and relax,' the old master said, opening a large blue door. 'Please help yourself to coffee and cupcakes. When ready problem, though . . .'

'What?'

'I'm busting to go to the loo!'

the ceiling?'

Josh pulled the wrapper off. 'Hey, shall I eat one
too, and see if the same thing happens to me?'

Charlie flapped his arms again. 'No, no,
don't . . . just in case there is something weird
going on with the cupcakes.'

Mum sighed loudly. 'Oh, this is crazy. I'm
not going to have my son spend the rest of his
birthday party bouncing around the ceiling like
a balloon! I'm calling Dr Hamill right away. He
knows all about Charlie's special abilities – he'll
be able to figure out a cure for this loopy problem.'
She marched out of the room.

Charlie looked down at Josh. 'Hey, mate, sorry
about this, I didn't mean to spoil the party.'

Josh looked up. 'What do you mean? You
didn't spoil the party.' He passed up to Charlie a
party hat and whistle. 'Look – I can send up as
much food and fizzy drink as you want – and
if I turn the TV on its side – then we can still
watch Commander Ron's movie later on. We'll
be fine.'

Charlie frowned. 'There's just one massive

a furry cannonball!'

'What!!' Trixie leapt off the couch. 'You tried to kill my cat!!!' She lunged at Charlie – but suddenly Charlie vanished right before her eyes.

'Sorry, mate,' Josh apologised. 'I didn't have a choice.'

BANG BANG BANG BANG. Both doors to the waiting room shuddered as the henchman pounded heavily on them from the other side.

'Give yourself up, Zero Boy, you're surrounded!' came a booming voice from behind the large blue door.

Charlie whispered into Josh's ear. 'All right, Josh, I'm going to leave and nab the general now.' He paused for a moment. 'There's just one problem, though – how do I open the door without letting those goons in?'

Josh furrowed his brow momentarily. 'Hey – can you pass through doors when you're invisible, you know, like Slider Boy, can?'

Charlie frowned. 'Me? Pass through doors? I dunno . . . I've never tried it before.'

Josh tapped his watch. 'Now's a good time to find out!'

'Okay . . .' Charlie rushed over to the large blue door. He pressed his face into the wood and pushed hard. 'Huarghhh!!!' He groaned slowly, sinking into it. 'I think it's working—' But suddenly – **KERSMASH** – the door collapsed outwards and crashed to the ground, knocking the two henchmen behind it off their feet. 'Oops,' Charlie groaned. 'That didn't work!'

'You're really going to have to learn to control that strength of yours, Charlie,' said Josh, eyeing the two dazed goons warily.

Charlie leapt back to his feet. 'Quick, Josh, take Trixie and get out of here, while you've got the

BOY ZERO - INVISIBLE HERO?

CLOMP CLOMP CLOMP. The sound of henchmen's boots quickly thumped down the hallway towards the waiting room.

'Quick, lock the doors,' Charlie thundered.

Josh sprinted across to lock the orange door while Charlie secured the large blue door.

'Ohh . . . you guys are so lame,' Trixie moaned, lying back on the sofa and closing her eyes.

Charlie glared at his image on the TV screens. 'This is a disaster! The general can see my every move — I can't take him by surprise like I'd planned. What am I going to do now?'

Josh looked up at the security camera. 'Wait a minute . . . I know how you can still take him by surprise!'

'How?' Charlie moaned.

'Charlie – his cameras can't track you if they can't see you – just turn yourself invisible!'

Charlie's face lit up. '*Awesome idea!*' He closed his eyes. 'Okay, here goes . . . Uggggggggggghhh . . .' He strained, gritting his teeth and concentrating as hard as he could. But nothing happened. 'Josh, it's not working,' he wailed.

'Well, you did it that time we were being attacked by General Pandemonium's killer robot. How did you do it then?'

'Um, it just seemed to happen. I think I have to be in life-threatening danger for it to work!'

Josh jumped back and screamed. 'Oi, look out, there's a giant killer snake behind you!!!'

Charlie frowned. 'No, Josh, *real* life-threatening danger.'

Josh paused for a moment. 'Hey, I've got an idea . . .' He ran over to Trixie. 'Er, Trixie, I promised Charlie I wouldn't tell you this . . . but, did you know that this morning he nearly killed your cat. He blew him up into the sky like he was chance!' he screamed.

'Hurry!' Josh howled, grabbing Trixie's hand and leading her out the doorway. 'Follow me.'

Trixie flicked his wrist away, running ahead of him down the hallway. 'Don't hold my hand, you geek . . .'

'Go for it! Hide somewhere safe,' Charlie boomed. 'I'll take care of the general.'

'Okay!' Josh cried, speeding down the hallway and quickly disappearing out of sight.

The two henchmen slowly got back to their feet, gazing mystified at the apparently empty room. Charlie ran over and – **KERCLONKK** – cracked their heads together, knocking them unconscious.

'Didn't see that coming, did you?' he shouted angrily. 'That's for calling me Zero Boy!'

THE BiLLoWiNG BLAST
oF BuRNiNG BEANS

Charlie zoomed around a corner, headed through
two sets of doors and slipped into the auditorium.
Up on the stage his dad, unaware of the
unfolding drama in the background, was speaking
passionately about teamwork to the bored-looking
Zero G workers.

'In life, there are two types of workers – those
who can do things, and those who can't do things,'
he chirped. 'The key to success is to always make
sure that you do what you do if you can, but if
you can't, then don't do what you can't do or else
you'll end up doing what you don't want to do . . .
am I clear?'

A look of dazed confusion spread across the

audience.

While Dad continued, Charlie sneaked his way past the henchmen into the middle of the auditorium. He looked ahead and spotted the general located at the refreshments bar.

'Gotcha now, big nose,' he muttered under his breath.

He broke into a sprint, but as he ran he suddenly felt a violent cramp grip his belly. He pulled up on the spot. 'Oh no,' he grimaced. 'Not those bloomin' beans again!' He doubled over in pain and – **PHHHARRPPP** – let loose a deafening explosion from the back of his invisible shorts.

'Pardon me!' he cried, turning bright red with

embarrassment, and instantly became visible again.

WEOOWWWWWWW!!! Smoke alarms triggered and – **KERSPLOSH** – freezing cold water blasted down from the safety sprinklers. The henchmen fell about clutching their throats as a scorching cloud of gas blanketed the auditorium.

The gagging general rolled out from behind the refreshments bar and spotted Charlie. 'Not you again!!!' he shrieked, pulling out his laser pistol.

Charlie charged towards the groaning supervillain. 'All right, General, your number's up this time!' he boomed.

But just a few metres before he reached the general, Charlie skidded on a wet patch on the carpet and – **WOOSH** – went flying head over heels up into the air. **KERDONGGG** – he smacked face first into a concrete pillar and – **KEFLUMP** – thumped back down to the ground.

'Oww, my head!' he moaned as he blacked out.

CHARLIE AND THE CATASTROPHIC CUPCAKE CRISIS

Charlie woke up with a throbbing headache.

He was lying on the floor of a brightly lit room.

'What happened?' he dithered dizzily.

'Muhahahah . . .' The general leaned over him,

pointing a laser pistol in his face. 'You failed again – that's what happened, you snivelling little snot!'

'Oh no, tell me this is a nightmare,' Charlie whined woozily.

Lieutenant Kurse ran over. 'General Snowplough, sir, really I don't think Master Sushi would approve of the way you're treating the boy right now . . .'

The general glared at the lieutenant. 'Who cares what Master Sushi thinks any more . . .' He waved the pistol in the air. 'Thanks to him, the entire security of our operation has been put under serious threat. He invited that idiotic author in, and he didn't bother to check if he was going to bring his annoying friend Zero Boy with him, did he? Huh, who else has that egghead invited here today, the prime minister and his entire world security team? No, no, Master Sushi is history – we have a major crisis on our hands and that requires the skills of a ruthless, merciless supervillain to deal with it. So it's goodbye Snowflake and *hello* Pandemonium!'

The room fell silent.

'Hooray,' a reluctant cheer went up.

The general circled Charlie. 'Hah, look at you – you're still wearing that ridiculous shower curtain, aren't you? Honestly, you're a joke.'

Charlie looked up at the general. 'What are you going to do with me?' he gasped groggily.

General Pandemonium sneered. 'Hmmmm, how about I make you disappear for ever!'

Charlie groaned. 'H–how are you going to d–do that?'

The general reached into his top pocket and pulled out a cupcake. 'By making you eat this . . .'

Charlie sat up and pushed his hand away. 'Never – not in a million years.'

The general rocked back on his heels and laughed. 'All right, we'll soon see about that.' He whispered into his cufflink communicator. 'Sergeant Briggs, bring out the prisoners.'

WHIRR CLICK. A door opened and out rolled a large steel cage on wheels with Dad, Josh and Trixie trapped inside it.

'Josh!' Charlie bellowed, rising unsteadily to his feet.

Josh thrust his arm between the steel bars.
'Charlie – sorry, the general's goons nabbed us
a few minutes ago. We had this awesome hiding
place, but Trixie kicked me out because she said I
had nits . . .'

Dad pointed at the general. 'Hey – you there in
the black, the coffee guy, I demand you release me
immediately or else I'll be forced to write a strong
letter of complaint to the Society of Self-Help
Authors.'

The general scowled and shoved the pistol into

Charlie's neck. 'Okay, Zero Boy, you've got one minute to eat this cupcake or else your stupid friends here are going to be dunked into a pool of Guzarian juice filled with ravenous man-eating piranhas!'

Josh shook his fist. 'Charlie – don't listen to the big goober, he's just bluffing.'

The general bared his teeth at Josh. 'Huh, when your toes are being chewed off one by one, you'll know I'm not bluffing.'

He glared at Charlie, shoving the cupcake in his face. 'EAT!'

Just then Master Sushi burst into the room. 'NO, NO, NO!' he screamed at the top of his voice. 'Snowflake, put gun down now. Do not harm little boy in shower suit!'

The general rolled his eyes. 'Oh, no, doesn't this guy ever take a break?'

The old master trotted over to the general. 'What you do? Leave child alone. Are you out of mind? Have you forgotten all I have taught you so far?'

The general waggled his pistol at Master Sushi. 'Listen, buster, all that I have learned so far is that the most precious possession to me in the entire universe is now floating helplessly somewhere up in the sky!' He stomped his foot angrily. 'And I've also learned that you welcomed here with open arms that nasty little superhero, Zero Boy, who tried to kill us all with his poison gas attack!'

'Poison gas attack?' Charlie yelped. 'No, I just had too many beans . . .'

The general's eyes blazed. 'Master Sushi, I've had it up to here with your mumbo-jumbo, touchy-feely nonsense and your ridiculous training challenges. You are nothing more than a foul-breathed, badly dressed, weirdly freckled annoying little Oompa-Loompa wannabe, and I want nothing more to do with you ever again. You're fired!!'

'Fired?' Master Sushi gulped.

Dad piped up. 'Perhaps I can be of some help. It seems you two have some deep unresolved personal issues you need help working through?'

'Silence!' General Pandemonium raged. He leaned into his communicator. 'Throw the midget into the cage with the others!'

'No, no,' Master Sushi cried as two armed

guards approached him.

The general thrust the pistol back into Charlie's neck again. 'Okay, you've got ten seconds left!' he bellowed looking at his watch.

'Don't do it!' Josh hollered.

'Five . . . four . . . three . . .'

Charlie looked at Josh, Dad and Trixie. He gulped and stretched out his hand. 'Okay, okay, I'll do it,' he bleated.

'Good . . .' the general said, preening his moustache. He flicked a red lever and –
WHIRRRRR – the roof of the room slid back, revealing the clear blue sky above. He bent down and placed the cupcake in Charlie's hand.

'Have a nice flight,' he cackled.

Charlie closed his eyes and bit into the cupcake.

A SERIOUSLY SHOCKING SECRET

'Noooooooo!!!' Josh hollered.

Trixie scowled. 'What are you crying about, you baby?' she scoffed. 'He's just eating a stupid cupcake.'

Charlie gulped and swallowed the last bit of the cupcake. Suddenly his eyes rolled back in his head and he flipped upside down and – SWISHH – lifted off the ground.

Josh covered his eyes.

Dad gasped. 'Oh my word, he's going all loopy again!'

The general put the laser pistol back in its holster and cracked his knuckles. 'Good riddance, you snotty little sucker.'

Charlie sailed up towards the opening in the

roof, but as soon as he passed through it, he stopped ascending and hovered helplessly in mid-air.

'Oh, that's strange,' Lieutenant Kurse observed, peering upwards.

The general stamped his foot. 'Why isn't he floating away like the other superheroes did?'

Josh uncovered his eyes. 'Charlie, you're still here,' he hollered. 'Why haven't you disappeared into the distance yet?'

Charlie shrugged his shoulders. 'I dunno. Maybe it's because my flying powers aren't as good as those of the other superheroes. I don't think the cupcake has quite the same effect on me.'

The general exploded. 'Lieutenant Kurse – fix

this problem immediately. I don't want this drippy little dirt bag hanging above my head a moment longer!'

'Roger that, sir.' The lieutenant urgently whispered into his communicator. He looked up. 'Oh, and sir, what shall we do with the other prisoners, while I'm fixing this problem?'

The general coldly slid his finger across the base of his throat. 'Feed them to the piranhas. Those poor little devils haven't eaten in days.'

'NO! NO!' Master Sushi bellowed. 'You must not hurt Mr Jack. He is world-famous author . . .'

'Yes, I concur with this strange little man,' Dad howled.

Josh pushed his face up against the bars. 'Hero Boy – do something!' he shouted. 'Save us now or we're all doomed. Can't you use your other powers?'

'Nothing seems to work any more,' wailed Charlie. 'It must be because of whatever's in the cupcake.'

Suddenly Trixie let out a deafening roar. She gripped the steel bars with her bare hands and –

FOARGGHHHH – tore them apart like they were chopsticks. She leapt out of the cage, grabbed the general and – **KERTHUDD** – slammed him head-first into the concrete floor.

'I said I'm bored and I want to go home NOW!' she thundered, pounding him up and down like a jackhammer. She then grabbed the top of his undies and – **WWRiPPPPPPP** – yanked them up over his head, giving him a super-wedgie.

'Owwwwwhhhh!!!' the general wailed in crippling agony.

Charlie's jaw dropped in astonishment. 'What the . . . ?' he shrieked from above. 'Trixie – y-you have superpowers too?'

WOOSH! Trixie flew up through the hole in the roof and grabbed Charlie out of the sky and pulled him back down to the ground again.

'S-since when did this happen?' he stuttered.

'Since my last birthday . . . I just woke up one morning and I felt really, really strong.' Trixie tied Charlie's cape around a table leg to stop him floating away.

Charlie was gobsmacked. 'This is unbelievable. Who would've thought it – two superheroes in the *same* family.' He stared at Trixie. 'Hey, you and me could form a super crime-fighting team!'

Trixie scowled. 'Are you nuts? I never want to be a superhero,' she growled. 'Superheroes are dorks. Have you seen the stupid costumes they have to wear? Uh-uh, no way, not me. I'll never be one of those dweebs.' She pulled her hair back in a pony tail. 'When I leave school, I'm going to be a fashion designer.'

Dad and Josh jumped out of the hole in the cage.

'I think I'm in love . . .' Josh glowed.

Dad hugged Trixie. 'Sweetie cakes, that was *sensational*. What on earth made you act so bravely?'

Trixie tapped her watch. 'My second-favourite programme, *Extreme Princess Makeover*, is on in twenty minutes – and there's no way that big-nosed egghead over there is going to make me miss it!'

The general staggered to his feet and painfully unhooked his poodle-themed pants from the tip of his huge nose. 'Uhhh . . . where am I?' he moaned dizzily. Charlie pulled the laser pistol out of his holster and pointed it at his face.

'You're in a whole heap of trouble, that's where you are, freak-face!'

The general groaned and reluctantly thrust his arms above his head.

'So what are we going to do with him?' Josh wailed. 'We can't send him back to jail – he might escape again.'

Charlie grinned. 'Hmmmm, how about we send him somewhere there's absolutely no chance of him ever escaping from again . . .'

'Where?' Josh cried.

'The deep, dark depths of outer space.' Charlie grinned, pointing his pistol at a pile of cupcakes stacked against one wall. 'Okay, big nose, get chomping!' he chuckled. 'And don't stop until I say you've had enough.'

Josh laughed and gave Charlie a high five.

The general cursed and ranted clenching his

fists. 'Noooo . . . this isn't happening. Nooooo. I'm ruined. That little pinhead has completely foiled my plans for world domination again. Arghhh!!' He slammed his forehead up and down on the table. 'I can't take any more of this . . .'

Lieutenant Kurse scooted over and quickly pulled a pen and piece of paper out of his pocket. 'Excuse me, sir,' he whispered. 'I don't mean to interrupt, but do you think now might be a great time to write another haiku?'

SAYONARA, MASTER SUSHI

Two days, four cans of baked beans and six cans of super-strength air-freshener later, Charlie was back home again, relaxing on his couch playing his favourite PlayStation game.

Josh, sitting next to him, turned up the sound on the television.

'Hey, look: they're launching the space mission to rescue the superheroes,' he buzzed. 'I bet you're jealous you can't go along with them.'

Charlie shook his head. 'Uh-uh, me on a spaceship packed full of baked beans? No way.' He pinched his nose. 'Besides, I wouldn't want to be anywhere near Commander Ron and the rest of those superheroes when the beans start taking

effect. Talk about serious global warming!'

'I'll say!' Josh nodded. He turned the TV off.

'Did they ever find the pop stars from Chubba Chubba Island?' asked Charlie.

'Yep,' replied Josh. 'They found them floating over an airfield in Texas. Apparently the air traffic controller thought they were part of a hot-air balloon display until he saw Lady Choc Bar pulling some of her dance moves in the sky, trying to signal for help.'

Charlie grinned.

'Hey,' said Josh. 'How do you think the general will be feeling right now, after eating all those cupcakes?'

Charlie chortled loudly. 'Hah, I'd say he'd probably be feeling over the moon . . .'

Just then Trixie burst into the room. 'Okay, gimme that,' she growled, snatching the PSP out of Charlie's hands.

'Hey, but I'm on a high score, Trixie!'

Trixie sneered. 'So what? Who cares? We have a deal, remember?' She strutted off. 'Oh, and my dishes need washing up now too,' she sniggered.

Josh groaned. 'Ooff, that's harsh! You're fresh back from saving the world, and this is how you're thanked?'

Charlie shrugged his shoulders. 'Don't worry, Josh – it's no big deal, honestly. I've got it sorted.'

Suddenly the front door swung open and in walked a short frail old man wearing a robe.

Josh leapt back on his seat. 'Quick, run . . . it's General Pandemonium's evil sidekick – that Mister Sushi guy!'

Charlie smiled and waved at the old man. 'Josh – relax, Mister Sushi's on our side now. After we saved him from the piranhas, he's taken a vow of goodness and promised never to do evil again.'

'Really?' Josh gasped.

'Yep.'

Master Sushi bowed. 'Ah, son of Mr Jack – I have cleaned four cars already today. Make much money for you.'

'Awesome,' Charlie cried.

Josh sat up. 'Huh, he's cleaning cars for you?'

Charlie grinned. 'Yeah, he's running a car wash to help raise money to buy me a new PSP. It's all part of his punishment for being evil over the last few years. He's actually really handy with a sponge too.'

'Son of Mr Jack – do you have any more chores for Master Sushi to do now?'

'Um, yep, I do. Apparently there's a whole lot of

dishes that need doing in the kitchen . . .'

Master Sushi bowed politely. 'Very good. I go and do them now. Then I go and wash more cars.'

'Brilliant.' Charlie jumped off the couch. 'Okay – now that I'm fully back to normal again, and all my chores are under control, I reckon it's time to do some serious skateboarding. What do you think, Josh?'

Josh jumped up. 'Absolutely.'

Charlie jogged towards the door. On his way he stopped and tapped Master Sushi on the shoulder. 'Oh, and by the way, did you manage to take care of that other little job I asked you about before?'

Master Sushi nodded and laughed quietly. 'Ha-ha, yes, I take good care of special job.'

'What job?' Josh hummed.

'You'll see,' Charlie chuckled. 'Come on, let's get out of here.'

Charlie and Josh ran out the front door and jumped onto their skateboards. As they whizzed down the garden path, suddenly – **KERTHUMP** – a deafening noise came from the upstairs bathroom. A few seconds later Trixie thrust her head out the window and screamed manically.

'Charlie!!!' she bellowed at the top of her lungs.
'Which one of you idiots put Vaseline on the toilet
seat?!!!'

EPILOGUE

Thousands of metres above the Applejack household, a sinister beak-like nose pierced through a layer of giant puffy white clouds. General Pandemonium shook his fist angrily as he helplessly floated further and further away from the earth.

Squinting in disbelief, he looked up and spotted what looked like a poodle-shaped cloud ahead of him in the distance.

He slowly opened his mouth and desperately cried out. 'M-miffy W-wiffy is that you, sweetie-poo pie?'

At first there was no response. But a few moments later, a tiny faint sound rang out . . .

'. . . *Ruff-ruff.*'

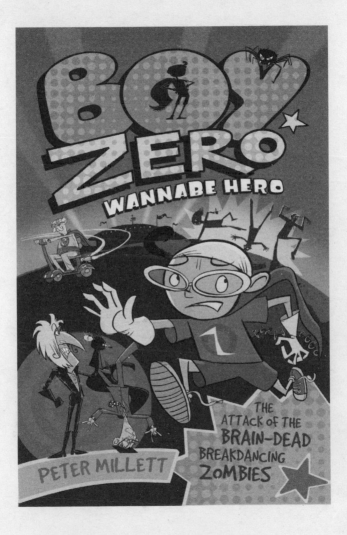